BECOMING **EXTRAORDINARY**

Becoming MARGARET LENG TAN

The Toy Piano Virtuoso Who Couldn't Stop Counting

Low Lai Chow
Illustrated by Dan Kuah

1945 was an important year.
World War II came to an end.
And Margaret Leng Tan was born.

Nobody knew, but Margaret had a secret. She could not just BE. Her obsessive-compulsive disorder (OCD) wanted her attention. ALL. THE. TIME.

It told her to straighten the bow in her hair.

It told her to count her steps on the stairs.

It told her to do this.
It told her to do that.
It just never stopped talking.

Margaret heard it all.
And she did as she was told.

Her parents finally said, "Okay."
And Margaret began to play her heart out.

She was UNSTOPPABLE.

Counting beats in music helped Margaret put OCD in its place, though it never went away. At 16, she won a scholarship to study piano at Juilliard, the most famous performing arts school in the world.

But one afternoon while watching the sun glinting on the East River, Margaret saw her future fill with light — and it was mighty bright!

Just like that, her homesickness fell away like petals in the wind.

She vowed to herself: *I am going to conquer New York. I am going to be famous.*

Margaret never looked back. In 1971, she became the first woman AND the first Singaporean to graduate with a doctorate from Juilliard.

History was being made. And Margaret was making it!

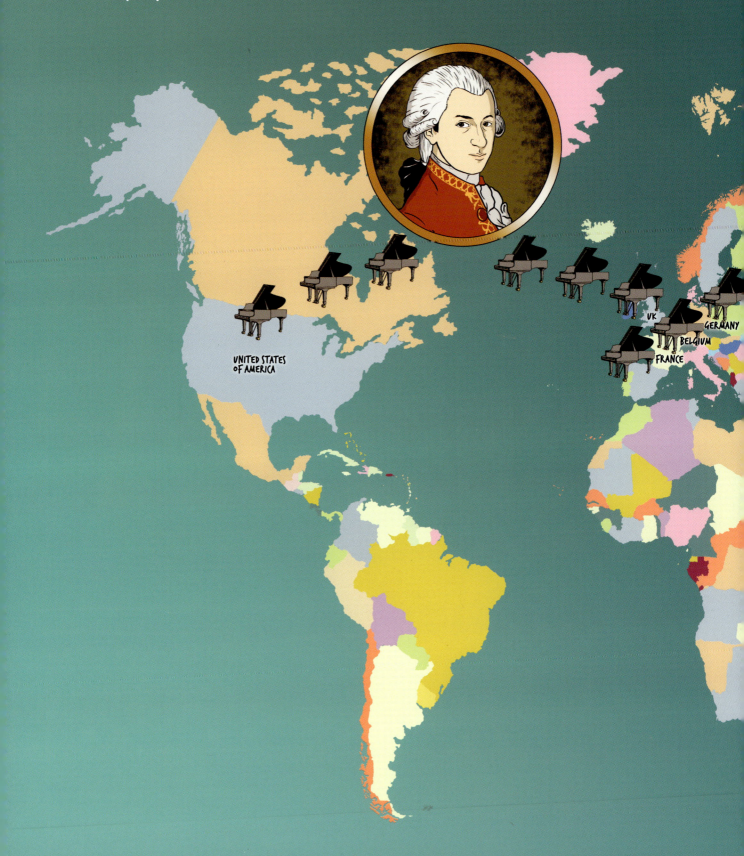

Her OCD was her constant companion. Sometimes it was SO LOUD, Margaret could not hear herself think.

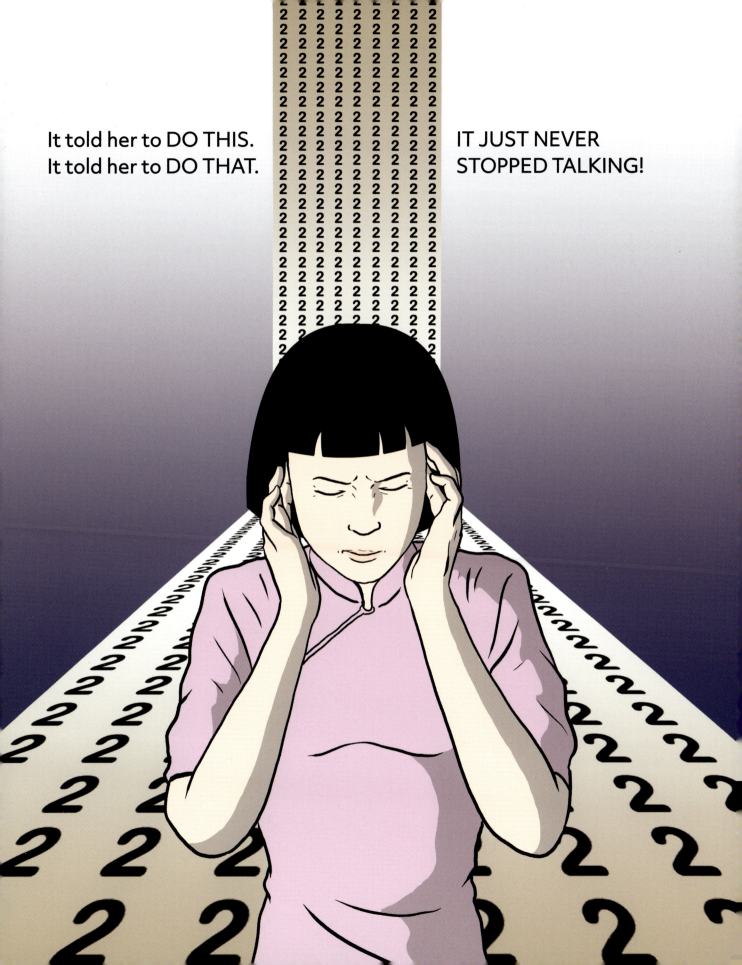

For a while Margaret stopped playing. Since she loved animals, she trained hearing dogs for the deaf instead.

But the music in her never went away.

After John Cage died in 1992, Margaret bought a toy piano and played it in tribute to him at New York's Lincoln Center.

PLINK! PLONK! The tiny toy piano came to life as a REAL instrument!

Margaret arranged her favourite classical melodies for the toy piano.

Her composer friends wrote toy piano pieces for her.

Margaret had magically transformed into the world's first CONCERT TOY PIANIST!

She actually had a hit album, *The Art of the Toy Piano*!

The New York Times hailed Margaret as the "Queen of the Toy Piano"!

Even the famous George Crumb wrote Margaret a piece. It was named *Metamorphoses (Book I)*, and she got to play the adult piano and the toy piano together AND go "CAW! CAW!" like a crow.

To top it all, Peanuts creator Charles M. Schulz wrote to Margaret upon hearing her album:

"I am very flattered that you have joined Schroeder as one of the great toy piano performers of all time"!

As if that wasn't enough, Margaret was invited to perform Beethoven ON TOY PIANO at Beethoven's house in Bonn, Germany!

Being a toy pianist was hard work but fun. People loved the sound of the toy piano because it reminded them of their childhood.

In 2002, Margaret played at Carnegie Hall. The seats were filled. Margaret was the first Singaporean to make it to Carnegie Hall's main stage!

In 2015, she received the Cultural Medallion, Singapore's highest honour for artists.

Margaret was amazed and amused that a toy pianist could receive such an award!

One bright August afternoon in 2022, four months before her 77th birthday, the light suddenly went out in Margaret's left eye.

But Margaret did not weep.
Why? Because DRAGON LADIES DON'T WEEP!

Her mind said, "*Is this the end? How will I play?*"

Without missing a beat her heart said, "*No. There must be a way. Just play.*"

And she did.

Margaret was, in fact, UNSTOPPABLE.

She went on, playing to entranced audiences.
She went on, playing to standing ovations.
She went on, playing to rave notices.
She went on, playing without anyone knowing
the secret about her eye… UNTIL NOW!

Oh, Margaret! Will she ever stop playing?
Luckily for us: NO!

Discussion Questions

- Imagine meeting Margaret in person one day. If you could ask her anything, what would it be?

- How would you feel if you couldn't stop counting? What would you do?

- What do you think the word "virtuoso" means?

- How does one become a piano virtuoso?

- Look around your room and pick the first item you see. If you could invent a new use for it, what would it be?

- If you could become really good at one thing, what would it be? How would you become REALLY good at it? List three actions you could take.

Who Is Margaret Leng Tan?

Margaret Leng Tan is the world's first toy piano virtuoso. She has had obsessive-compulsive disorder (OCD) since she was a little girl. However, confronting the daily challenges posed by OCD has never stopped her from accomplishing great things in art and in life. In 2015, she received the Cultural Medallion, Singapore's highest artistic award. Margaret continues to reinvent herself to this day, starring as herself in her theatre play, *Dragon Ladies Don't Weep*, and speaking out for animal rights through her toy piano performances. She lives in New York with her dogs. Margaret is pure inspiration for us all!

Scan here to learn more about Margaret Leng Tan.

You might also like:

Dragon Ladies Don't Weep

Twinkle Dammit!

Sorceress of the New Piano

CNN Great Big Story

Curios

She Herself Alone: The Art of the Toy Piano 2

Songs for Unusual Creatures: Jesus Christ Lizard

Front cover illustration created from a photograph by Jim Standard.

Special thanks and gratitude to:

Margaret Leng Tan whose guidance and inspiration made this book possible; Jeannie Schulz and Charles M. Schulz Creative Associates for Schroeder's participation; José García-León, Dean of Academic Affairs at The Juilliard School, for advice on Juilliard commencement attire and Jeni Dahmus-Farah, Director of Archives, for facilitating access to the Juilliard Archives;

The following individuals and institutions whose photographs were the source for many of the illustrations: David Andrako, Evans Chan, Christopher Chew, Michael Dames, Michael Davidson, George Hirose, Wojtek Kornet, Susana Lei'ataua, Connie Marder, Jack Vartoogian; Mode Records, CultureLink Singapore, Yong Siew Toh Conservatory of Music (Singapore), National Arts Council, Singapore, Esplanade – Theatres on the Bay (Singapore);

Nick Roux, whose video projections in the production, *Dragon Ladies Don't Weep*, co-produced by Chamber Made (Melbourne) and CultureLink Singapore and co-commissioned by Esplanade – Theatres on the Bay (Singapore) and Asia TOPA (Melbourne), inspired the illustrations on pages 16–19; Charles M. Schulz Creative Associates and Peanuts Worldwide LLC for graciously allowing the inclusion of Schroeder's image on page 29;

The following institutions and individuals for their kind permission to include Margaret Leng Tan's posters: Esplanade – Theatres on the Bay (Singapore), The Library of Congress (Washington D.C., USA), Oz Asia Festival (Adelaide, Australia), National Performing Arts Centre/Performing arts redefined (Par magazine) (Taipei, Taiwan), Evans Chan and Chuang Xu;

Wise Music Group for permitting the reproduction of the book cover of *Schirmer's Library of Musical Classics Vol 2056 CHOPIN, Complete Preludes, Nocturnes and Waltzes* on page 8 and Steinway & Sons for permitting the use of the Steinway logo on page 31.

© 2023 Marshall Cavendish International (Asia) Pte Ltd

Published by Marshall Cavendish Children
An imprint of Marshall Cavendish International

All rights reserved

No part of this publication may be reproduced, stored in a retrieval system or transmitted, in any form or by any means, electronic, mechanical, photocopying, recording or otherwise, without the prior permission of the copyright owner. Requests for permission should be addressed to the Publisher, Marshall Cavendish International (Asia) Private Limited, 1 New Industrial Road, Singapore 536196. Tel: (65) 6213 9300
E-mail: genref@sg.marshallcavendish.com
Website: www.marshallcavendish.com

The publisher makes no representation or warranties with respect to the contents of this book, and specifically disclaims any implied warranties or merchantability or fitness for any particular purpose, and shall in no event be liable for any loss of profit or any other commercial damage, including but not limited to special, incidental, consequential, or other damages.

Other Marshall Cavendish Offices:
Marshall Cavendish Corporation, 800 Westchester Ave, Suite N-641, Rye Brook, NY 10573, USA • Marshall Cavendish International (Thailand) Co Ltd, 253 Asoke, 16th Floor, Sukhumvit 21 Road, Klongtoey Nua, Wattana, Bangkok 10110, Thailand • Marshall Cavendish (Malaysia) Sdn Bhd, Times Subang, Lot 46, Subang Hi-Tech Industrial Park, Batu Tiga, 40000 Shah Alam, Selangor Darul Ehsan, Malaysia.

Marshall Cavendish is a registered trademark of Times Publishing Limited

National Library Board, Singapore Cataloguing in Publication Data

Name(s): Low, Lai Chow. | Kuah, Dan, illustrator.
Title: Becoming Margaret Leng Tan : the toy piano virtuoso who couldn't stop counting / Low Lai Chow ; illustrated by Dan Kuah.
Other Title(s): Becoming extraordinary.
Description: Singapore : Marshall Cavendish Children, [2023]
Identifier(s): ISBN 978-981-5084-91-7 (hardback)
Subject(s): LCSH: Tan, Margaret Leng--Juvenile literature. | Pianists--Singapore--Biography--Juvenile literature. | Obsessive-compulsive disorder--Juvenile literature.
Classification: DDC 786.2092--dc23

Printed in Singapore